MADAME VERONA
COMES DOWN THE HILL

Born in Belgium in 1972, DIMITRI VERHULST is the author of a collection of short stories, a volume of poetry and several novels. In 2009 he was awarded the Libris Prize in the Netherlands.

DAVID COLMER is an Australian writer and translator. He has won several translation awards, including the NSW Premier's Translation Prize.

From the international reviews of
Madame Verona Comes Down the Hill:

'A delightful oddity of a book... written in a quirky style [that] manages to be witty, wise and moving.' *Waterstone's Books Quarterly*

'A brilliantly eccentric fable... Verhulst is a writer of great charm, his tale of grief snaking its way effortlessly between the ludicrous and the poignant.' *Age* (Melbourne)

Madame Verona Comes Down the Hill

Dimitri Verhulst

TRANSLATED FROM THE DUTCH
BY DAVID COLMER

BOOKS

First published by Portobello Books Ltd 2009
This paperback edition published 2010

Portobello Books Ltd
12 Addison Avenue
London
W11 4QR

First published in Dutch in 2006 as *Mevrouw Verona daalt de heuvel af*
by Uitgeverij Contact, the Netherlands

A CIP catalogue record is available from the British Library

2 4 6 8 9 7 5 3 1

ISBN 978 1 84627 157 1

www.portobellobooks.com

Text designed and typeset by Patty Rennie
Printed and bound in Great Britain
by CPI Bookmarque, Croydon

For Nathalie, at last

My dog is old. When he is in pain, an imploring look comes into his eyes. I am his God. He doesn't know that behind the God that will save him, the one he beseeches, there is another God he cannot see. Is there another behind ours as well? The dog grovels at my feet. At whose feet must we grovel?

JEAN RAY

I

Somewhere, in one of the many narrative repositories that have been set up here and there for us to draw on when the world needs a story, it must be possible to find the fable that tells us that people, on their arrival in the realm of the dead, must lay claim to a trait, one only, that characterizes the life they have just led. After all, we need to be able to imagine the afterworld as a pleasant place – that's a precondition of these fables, and you would have to be quite naïve to believe that an eternal sojourn in a single location with everyone who has ever and will ever die could remain pleasant for very long. According to the fable in question, the wandering souls are grouped according to shared characteristics, from which we can immediately conclude that it must be especially busy in those parts of the hereafter that are filled with people who strove during their lifetime to accumulate as much money as possible, possess fire, become a famous guitarist, famous in any discipline at all, or where the resurrected population consists of all those who let their self-esteem depend on the number of their amorous conquests.

Of course, this fable about the hereafter is actually a fable about life, which is why even notorious atheists can derive a great deal of pleasure from considering it as a hypothetical situation. On that icy day in late February, for instance, Madame Verona thought about what she would shortly confess to eternity's fabled gatekeeper as the chief characteristic of the life that had surrendered its last toehold and was now slipping away from her. It wasn't so much that she was thinking about *what* to tell him – she had no doubts on that score – it was *how to put it* that bothered her.

*

The one characteristic element with which she would summarize her eighty-two years of existence was that dogs had always sought out her company. There must have been something about her, even when she was very young, that made dogs feel safe around her. As a girl she was often snuffled by passing quadrupeds that immediately begged to be patted, offering to shake hands the way ridiculous people had taught them to. Even more intelligent breeds known for their distrust of children caught a whiff of whatever it is that makes dogs wag their tails, and guard dogs that had been trained to foam at the mouth at the sight of a stranger abandoned all xenophobia in her presence. In the summer, when many a holidaymaker dumped the family pet on a convenient roadside, she encountered starving dog after starving dog, and would have taken them all home with her if not for the presence there of a mother who could scream entire octaves at the mere thought of a dog. The only thing her mother had ever permitted her was a childish or, more accurately, girlish dedication to guinea pigs, and even then mother dear would have probably suffered a heart attack if one of the creatures had ever escaped its cage. And there was no question of a mother like hers being able to sympathize with the immature grief of a child digging a hole in the back garden to accommodate the shoe or cigar box that would be lowered into it after the last rites that only children administer to dead animals.

Madame Verona had not seen her parental home since the day her mother was lowered into that same merciful earth, after which the house was sold to people who showed no interest in the history of their new dwelling. But if she had just once succumbed to a nostalgic impulse to sniff up the atmosphere of her tender years, she could have strolled through the garden knowing it was rooted in a small animal cemetery. It was highly unlikely that anything would be left of the countless cavy cadavers or the birds that had ended up there after leaving a greasy spot on a windowpane, but with a little effort she could have recalled which animal was sleeping the sleep of sleeps under which shrub. More than that, she could have remembered what all those little creatures had been called: Mimi, Cuddles, Fluffy, Skittles, Bill, Dolly, or whatever names thirteen-year-old girls give their pets and later feel a mistaken sense of embarrassment about.

Nonetheless, in the case of Madame Verona, we should differentiate between a relatively standard love of animals and the power over dogs she enjoyed throughout her life. Although it is questionable whether 'enjoyed' is the right word in this context. After stubbornly bringing yet another pitiful stray home with her (wrong again: she didn't *bring* them, the dogs simply followed her), she endured her mother's predictably hysterical outburst and then delivered the animal in question to the shelter, realizing that imprisonment there was the price of a full stomach and hoping against hope that this dog might be adopted by wiser owners. That last bit is a figure of speech, as it is common knowledge that there is absolutely no point in buying or adopting a dog in the hope of calling yourself its owner; it's always the dog that chooses the owner, even if that means waiting patiently for rain to rust the chain and long days spent marching.

It is hard to say when exactly Madame Verona first became aware of her abnormal appeal for dogs, but she was around twenty when she travelled independently for the first time and ascertained that her peculiarity was just as potent in foreign countries. Of course, many people have been tickled by an unsolicited offer of simple canine friendship and honoured by an animal showing up to present itself as a confidant, even if it's almost always more trouble than it's worth.

She, for instance, suddenly found herself with a sheepdog as *compagnon de route* on a hiking trip through Portugal. The dog asked nothing of her, he simply followed along behind, days on end, through and over the gentle hills around Coimbra. At night, under the stars, he stretched out on the hard ground that bent her tent pegs, and in the morning he simply resumed *her* path, after first stretching his front legs in an ancient yawn that displayed every last one of his rotten yellow stalactites and stalagmites. He made no attempt to demand a share of her meals. And she didn't give him anything either, hoping he would go back to wherever he had come from. Puddles were all he needed and, fortunately, there were plenty of those. Finally, a couple of weeks and many miles later, a stone's throw from Porto airport, knowing she couldn't take him home with her, she rejected him with a pointing finger and feigned anger that didn't come close to convincing him. Then, for the first time, he let her hear his bark, and the sound cut her to the bone. It was a paltry, worn-out yap, no longer capable of impressing even a sheep. Then he turned, in all his loneliness, hoping that a destination would reveal itself.

*

When Madame Verona's thoughts turned to the fable on that cold day in February, another dog was lying at her feet, the kind of farm dog that Renaissance painters cursed for the way the subtle gradations of colour in its coat revealed the copyist's limitations as a Creator, the mass breeding of which must have stopped sometime in the mid-nineteenth century. A magnificent animal with leadership qualities, gentle through and through, but inclined to boredom. She had vacillated before letting him in, considering her age, but the requests people cannot resist are never asked, they are in the eyes, like the melancholy sub-servient eyes with which he had stared up at her until she said, 'Fine, come in, you can live here, but you'd better realize you're going to survive me, so don't get too attached.'

The hour at which the dog would be obliged to seek a new master was approaching, and his legendary intuition was undoubtedly making him uneasy. But for the time being he didn't let that show and lay on the cooling feet of Madame Verona, who thought, 'This is what I'll say when I get up there – that I've always been popular with dogs.' And it occurred to her that her beloved husband, Monsieur Potter, who had preceded her to the realm of fables, had probably said the very same thing to death's concierge. He too had always had dogs at his heels. And what could be more logical than Madame Verona and Monsieur Potter being reunited in the terrifying emptiness known as The World to Come? Their being accommodated in different sections of the hereafter would make a mockery of beauty.

II

If we took a topographic map and tried to visualize the slopes of the village of Oucwègne, the contours would remind a novice map-reader of a funnel, whereas a seasoned scout would settle for a drain: a gutter in the earth's crust, worn away with immense patience by a river. Because that's what rivers seem to do, they cut the earth into pieces and take billions of years over it. The proximity of a river, a limited knowledge of the Bible and a little poetic licence... that was all the old church builders needed to dedicate the chapel in the valley to John the Baptist. But the power of faith never won out over the muscle power required to climb one of the three hills on the way home after Mass. On peak days, determined by dry weather and less slippery roads, the curé raised his chalice of consecrated Beaujolais to a maximum of six elderly women with well-turned calves, during a tinkling of bells that the congregation was obliged to imagine at the appropriate moments due to a lack of altar boys.

It's difficult to trace the origin of the misconception that people in small agrarian communities are more religious than their urban fellows, but it is possible that decades of the mass reproduction of Jean François Millet's *Angelus* have played a role that should not be underestimated. In Oucwègne, at least, churchgoers were scarcely to be found unless it was when the bells in the tower were pealing or tolling to spread the tidings of a wedding or funeral through the valley. Six practising faithful – it could have been seven if we weren't discounting someone like Jean-Paul, who dipped his hairy fingers in the holy water every week, but only attended Mass to accompany the quavering voices on his violin and thus assure himself of the thing he so desperately lacked as an interpreter of Bach's partitas: an audience. Of course, we cannot exclude the possibility of someone saying a paternoster now and then in bed, especially the insomniacs – given that the sedative effects of a Hail Mary are well known to all those who ever knitted their fingers together under the blankets as a pious child only to discover that the end of a decade of the rosary seldom arrived before dreamland. In any case, Curé Dubois, a former missionary with an incurable homesickness for the tropics, ignored all other suggestions and blamed the secularization in this unlamented corner of the world on the physical effort church attendance here required, not least of all from the elderly.

*

The three hills that made up the village were inaccessible during severe winters and each hill formed its own hamlet as long as there was a crunch in the snow: Biènonsart, Le Pachis and Chènia. It was on the top of that last hill that Madame Verona lived in a house that could have been lifted from a biscuit tin. And it was this hill that she had come down on that cold day in February, together with her friendly stray, legs wide apart to keep her balance and leaning on her stick, the third leg that was by far the strongest of the three. It was already late afternoon by the time she set out, after her catnap and a sandwich to keep her going. The sky had taken on the colour of an old mop and the birds on the branches were in congress about whether to stay or go, familiar harbingers of a long period of snow. And Madame Verona knew that she would never make it back home by herself – least of all 'on her own two legs', if that didn't sound too cynical for someone who depended on a walking stick. After making it down to the valley she looked up and saw from the chimney that the log she had put on the fire that morning was still burning.

If she ever wanted to make it back home, she had

little choice but to wait until someone came by in a car and offered her a lift. Considering the general friendliness of the region, that was something she could definitely count on, but the weather conditions suggested that hardly anyone would be venturing out at this hour. If no one came by – and this was something she had realized while coming down the hill – she would undoubtedly die here in the cold night, because she had no intention of once again resisting the dictatorship of the body. The last time she had climbed the hill on foot it had taken her hours and she had felt humiliated by her own bones. At the top, she had sworn never again to allow herself to be seduced into rebelling against old age, something that could only lead to snooty airs and, on another level, had already driven countless others into the arms of the pharmaceutical industry. They were out there, the people who believed that eternal youth was an ingredient in a particular brand of yogurt and almost made a sacrament of anointing themselves with the most disgusting kinds of grease as an antidote to the ailments of the years, trying to live without leaving a trail in the testimony of their skin. The trees had their rings; Madame Verona did not begrudge her skin its wrinkles, the signature of all her days.

*

'I could die here,' she had said so many years earlier, after seeing the house for the first time with her beloved Monsieur Potter and discussing whether or not to buy it. As if death allowed anyone or anything to impose geographical limitations. They stood together in the living room where they would later put the bed, since it faced east and great lovers like to admire each other by the first, almost tentative, light of day. They had opened the window, looked out over the hilltops, the distant farms and fields where patient cows grazed their dewlaps fatter to please their butchers. They saw the woods clinging fast to darkness, the clouds drifting in formation to their destinations, and the viaduct that stretched across the valley a little further along to make it easier to get from the commotion of one big city to another. Below them the river described its path in calligraphic curls, graceful majuscules whose existence people had almost forgotten since the introduction of the keyboard. And while they looked at that landscape, they wondered whether in the long run they would be able to withstand its simple beauty, or whether they would be swept away by the solitude of these surroundings.

There was their house and there was Oucwègne. Full of villagers they didn't know, who dared to live hermetic lives, if the stories told by city-dwellers could be believed. It would be a leap in the dark. 'I could die here,' she said, and Monsieur Potter lit a cigarette at the window and rested his gaze on a host of ancient trees whose bark provided a winter home for as yet unfamiliar insects. 'Absolutely,' he replied, 'this is a house you could die in and it's a house you could be unhappy in. We'd be mad not to take it.'

As peculiar as his line of reasoning may seem, there is something instructive about it. Someone who is buying a house for life and is happy has to realize that sooner or later unhappiness could rear its head. In the form of disease, old age, whatever. So yes, the question people need to ask when buying a house is, 'Can I be unhappy here too?' And he meant that this landscape could absorb his bouts of melancholy better than any other. They were growing less common, those bouts, perhaps because they were more in keeping with a certain youthfulness he had gradually left behind, but he still preferred to take them into account. A leap in the dark, to tumble into light. 'We'll buy it,' and they filled the empty room with the echoing cries of their lovemaking, smoothed the creases out of their clothes and drove to the notary's office.

A smile appeared on Madame Verona's face as she thought back on it. A curve in thin lips, a single bracket concluding a long, beautiful sentence. A memory of happiness that, in a more wistful key, could also be called happiness.

III

In winter the heart of Oucwègne was located in the former Catholic cinema, a decrepit building with walls still damp from the days when people let out deep, tubercular sighs at the sight of Greta Garbo and Humphrey Bogart – when their deceptive, angelic faces slipped in under the guard of the censorship committee, at least. The silver screen had been carted off after it swelled up from an excess of dark yellow tobacco fumes – which was why the last black-and-white films shown here appeared in sepia – but the suffering of the tormented bricks resumed when

Cécile de la Charlerie started using the place to cook innumerable cauldrons of mussels in aid of this, that or the other. Garlic mussels, mussels in white wine, all kinds of mussels, served with chips and meatballs smothered with a ladleful of tomato sauce; meals that aroused a suspicion of inviolable happiness and demonstrated why the papists had made the Eucharist the core of every gathering. Our stomachs were the first to figure it out: it's not the meeting, it's the eating that brings people closer to God.

But most of all it was Gordon who breathed new life into the canteen of the old cinema by volunteering to man the bar for a few hours each week. It was true that the disappearance of the last café had not shattered social relations completely; everyone had a set of pétanque balls and shared the bottles they brought from home on the village square under the plane tree. While cheerfully getting drunk and watching their balls come to rest further and further from the jack, they got bites on the lines they had thrown here and there into the river, and later they grilled the fish and ate them with their fingers, spitting the bones out on the ground almost irreverently. But that was in the summer, when it was so hot that pear rust broke out and red spider mite in the glasshouses ruined half of the cucumber harvest, the kind of warmth that made it possible for people to spend the night comfortably outdoors when they were too drunk to attempt the climb home. Madame Verona and Monsieur Potter, too, only needed a single party to realize how difficult it was to climb the hill with beery legs. They stumbled uphill as if on the road to Emmaus, but were content at feeling immediately accepted by all of the biggest mouths in the village.

Gloriosas were growing through all of the good memories and the cinquefoil flowered peach. You noticed it in the elation with which they built an imposing tower of dead spruce in March and set fire to it to welcome spring: winter was tough here, lonely above all, and, as long as the embers glowed, those who had come through it drank jenever to make sure they forgot it as soon as possible. That was why Gordon opened the canteen of the cinema during the darkest months. It wasn't a lot. A bar, a fridge. And a basic record player with a maximum volume that people easily drowned out when singing along to the songs of Charles Aznavour, him above all. In the corridor to the pisser there was a plaster Jesus whose plausibility was enhanced by his missing fingers: they made Him someone from here, someone like Tosh, a man fathers used as an example when initiating their sons into the workings of the chainsaw. And, together with a few tables and chairs and a train station clock, we have now covered the building's entire inventory. Wait – we've forgotten the most important thing of all – the table-football table.

The canteen was a clubhouse more than a bar: it didn't keep fixed opening hours and there were no mercantile goals to explain Gordon's flouting of the laws regarding public drunkenness. But if there was one surety in this boozer's shadowy existence, it was the fact that it was a meeting place where the locals gathered every Sunday morning to boast about the number of pheasants shot and strew superlatives about harvests and excess stock.

One of the people who accepted drinks there was Robert, an elderly man who felt naked without his trilby and wore it everywhere except to funerals. After pulling up a chair at his regular table, he always put his box of cigars down in front of him. The cigars were cheap and nasty, inferior tobacco rolled in leaves that gave off more smoke than aroma. The box bore the portrait of a podgy king in nylon stockings, after whom the cigars had also been named, and it was for Robert alone that Rosetta Courthéoux stocked a supply of these unpalatable fumigators in her grocery store; there was no one else in the whole area who would consider taking as much as a puff of this brand, no matter how severe the cigarette shortage. There was something masochistic about Robert putting the cigars down in front of him, as he had marked each cigar band with the exact lighting-up time. The same phenomenon is seen in avid smokers who have started suffering sudden pain in their upper back but prefer to limit consumption instead of quitting entirely, but their motives are undoubtedly different. It was not fear of modern diseases that compelled Robert to time his smoking, but stinginess. He rationed himself solely to avoid exceeding his allotted monthly expenditure. You could say that he had put himself on a diet, even if dieticians generally prefer to keep nicotine outside their area of expertise. And so Robert laid his cigars on the table, eavesdropped on conversations and kept a careful eye on the clock. Everyone in Oucwègne was aware of his miserliness, but people saw it as a disease and never called him to account. They included Robert in the rounds they bought, and when logic pointed him out as the next to buy, no one committed a murder when he missed his turn or suddenly needed to go home.

Robert had reached an age at which it took him a good hour to come down the hill for his pints of beer, and there was no question of his returning home unaided. Once he had made it to the canteen, his problems were solved – he knew that there would be someone there to help him back up the hill. It was willpower and stubbornness and thirst that drove him in the end to descend backwards, leaning on the asphalt with his hands, just like a toddler coming down a staircase, and it must have been a terrible realization that each visit to the canteen could be his last. Because that day was approaching – his upper legs were already swinging like pendulums, shaking and creaking at the knees – and soon he wouldn't make it downhill. Not even like a toddler. It had always been a more or less inevitable event in his future, so he could have prepared himself, but still. Time had finished with him and the Sunday came when Robert was no longer sitting in the canteen. He was the first person whose tragedy made Madame Verona and Monsieur Potter realize that they too could one day become prisoners of the hill, and they were surprised by the laconic way in which the other regulars brushed aside their concern.

The last cigar Robert lit, months after his final

visit to the canteen, was the cigar from 2.10 p.m. His cigar bands had made it easy for Dr Lunette to be fairly exact when specifying the time of death. The hour, at least. For the date, she gave herself a margin of error of plus or minus ten days.

IV

Although his father had hanged himself from a branch at a relatively young age, Monsieur Potter was touchingly ignorant when it came to trees. He couldn't tell a beech from an oak and could just manage to distinguish a spruce and a pine, at least until the Christmas tree industry got involved and started growing all kinds of intermediary varieties, in bizarre colours as well. Of course, as a child, when the arrival of autumn prompted the headmaster to set poetic projects, he had put together the occasional herbarium, drawing up separate sections of exercise book for serrated and lobed, and noting the names of the trees under the corresponding leaves after first drying them for days on end all over the living room under piles of magazines and thick books. The colours of death had surprised and moved him as much as his youth allowed, but his arboreal knowledge never outlasted the herbarium itself. Willows, he could recognize. They were often solitary and polled, lonely but stubborn, standing up to the wind for years. The willow was a tree with the determination of a peasant, a will that could only be broken by a lightning bolt. He recognized weeping willows easiest, but that was because a teacher had once told him that this tree owed its name to the way its branches drooped, as if it were staring at the ground in sorrow while the others tried to claw the moon. The story annoyed him, because he had always thought of weeping willows as cheerful and graceful. Nothing like the pollard willow, his favourite – so different, in fact, that he found it bizarre that trees with such dissimilar characters could belong to the same family.

All this could give the impression that he actually did know something about trees, but he was still never able to tell us what kind of tree his father had hanged himself from. That was probably for the best, because otherwise he might have been unable to resist searching for associations and meanings that were possibly non-existent. For the sake of completeness, we should mention his knowledge of palm trees, which he mainly knew from movies and thought of as deformed pineapples.

Back then, all those years ago, when the notary unfolded the floor plan of their new house and handed them the details of the boundaries, it turned out that they also owned a neighbouring wood. It hadn't been mentioned in any of the advertisements or documents and they had been happy just living on its edge, but the wood was definitely included in the purchase price and now they were obliged to maintain it. Obliged? Privileged!

*

Four worthless and clearly reluctant roads connected the hill to the rest of world and, of these four, Madame Verona had chosen, on that February day, to come down the most difficult. The forest path, whose gradient and impassability were such that on weekends an array of idiots worked their way up it on mountain bikes, guys who were convinced that tormenting the body was the price death demanded for a long and limber life. When they finally reached the top they were pale and immediately began guzzling disgustingly colourful regenerative soft drinks, but the effort had undoubtedly given them the courage to sit through another week at a desk where the pot plants summoned up memories of the nature documentaries that consoled their atavism of an evening. Nostalgia for the smell of sweat had driven others into the arms of a hiking club, and they too parked their cars somewhere down in the village before embarking on the climb in footwear that was designed for long marches in the polar regions. The cameras they lugged up with them betrayed their predilection for the heroic, and not a hair on their heads realized that they were shooting their photos from under rain hoods like caricatures of nineteenth-century explorers. The local hunters wisely ignored the existence of this road full of cobbles that wobbled and were about to let loose completely in the saturated soil. After all, their bodies were empires built up over decades, with bellies like basilicas dedicated to the enticement of ladies who knew how to value a red-blooded man. Even one who alerted any game well in advance by his heavy breathing and the raucous way he hawked up the phlegm that was saturated with the tannins from last night's Pinot Noir.

Calendars had been stripped bare since the last time Madame Verona had set foot on the forest path, a place that more than anywhere else linked her with her husband. Childhoods are seldom happy, but here Monsieur Potter had found it easy to forget his quaggy past while rehabilitating diseased trees as firewood, with an axe at first but, after just a year, more realistically with a chainsaw. He had to slave to

do it, because the trees lay on a slope that was so slippery with mulch that he had to anchor himself to the
more reliable trunks with a hip belt. Afterwards he
had to drag the wood uphill, like a centaur made up
of an Ardennes draught horse and a much too thin
man, cut it into smaller pieces, split them, and stack
them according to precise rules he had picked up
from experienced locals. Fire was the primary fruit of
these trees and warmth was the harvest. After three
years' seasoning, the wood gave them the smell that
all gods undoubtedly use as a perfume and heat that
makes anything produced by electric devices look
like a joke. When the toppled giants were already
rotten he left them where they lay, fungi enveloped
the roots and worms did what they had been put on
earth to do: demolition. In open places he protected
the saplings from the ravenous deer, which he com-
pensated with hiding places made of the branches
he'd trimmed away. But even when he wasn't working, Monsieur Potter enjoyed being here, seeing the
aureoles force their way down through the foliage

and listening to the rustling wind, either alone or with Madame Verona, and sliding downhill with her on a sled, the winters telling him that lovers were children, trying to reach back into the past to seize the time they hadn't spent together. Wanting to have shared their entire lives with each other, because love refused to settle for less.

When he found out about his disease, Monsieur Potter resolved to fight one last battle: to stack as much wood as possible, providing his wife with warmth that came from him until she was old. The trees wept resin at his rampant chainsaw. Everything that was diseased, uprooted, blown over or strangled by ivy was split and cut down to size and the garden filled at an industrial tempo with solid walls of firewood. It had seemed like an inexhaustible supply, but that morning in February Madame Verona had laid the last log on the fire. The last piece of firewood that he too had held in his splinter-pierced hands. There had been less and less to hold that he too had held, because if things don't rot, they break, and when she pushed that last log deeper into the fire with the poker, she decided to go down the hill. As a symbol, a meaningless act set opposite a meaningless fact, but more beautiful.

*

Soon it will start to snow again and there will be no sled to leave its furrows in the white. She looked into the wood a last time and saw how, after her lover, it had gone back to arranging things the way it liked them. For years the wars between mosses and barks had been fought openly again, the elms died standing and furious roots churned the earth. Set on revenge, determined to retake the planet, re-establishing its logic-defying chaos, the wood had grown wild. And it was beautiful. *Man*: they should never have let him crawl up out of the water. Perhaps it was a parting kindness from her own mind, letting her think that final thought before dying herself.

V

I don't want you to wait when my time has come.
You can tuck me in, briefly, but that's more than
enough.
And if, while tucking me in, you smile a sweet smile,
just once I'll forgive you your feigned happiness.

Don't sit by my bed to count the erratic intervals
between my putrid breaths. Don't hold my hand,
which will lie there like a mitten that once contained
my hand that reached for yours.
Don't listen to the grisly pound and rattle

in my chest as cancer does its best
to reconstruct my bones
and don't look into my eyes,
broken in their sockets and adjusting
to the pitch dark of what will be no night.

Leave me behind in that room. Alone.
Because the two of us belong to life.

Please ignore this banality and go,
downstairs, into the garden.
Hang your dresses on the line and I will watch
through the window as they salute me in the wind.
Fry something, onions perhaps, and brown them well
in butter, so I can smell them here, upstairs,
and think, 'My God, she sure knows how to cook!'

But if my legs still hold,
and I hope they will,
I'll grip the banister
that still needs varnishing

and say, 'I'm already upstairs, sweetheart,
I'll see you in a bit.'

VI

As the nearest doctor's practice was in a neighbouring village, virtually the entire population of Oucwègne went to the vet's when ill. It wasn't as if there could be that much difference between a pig and a person anyway, not if the anatomical posters on the walls of Dr Lunette's waiting room could be believed, and anyone who refused to accept the similarities only needed to go down on all fours for a moment. A bag of gizzards with limbs attached, held together by slime and a skeleton. The cycle of scoffing and shitting took place in all bodies, higher and lower, the holes served the same filthy purposes and they all tasted more or less the same to the lice and ticks. There may have been occasional differences in the way the creatures divided their time between fucking and feeding, but they were all playgrounds for bacteria, cocci, bacilli and spirilla, they had the same glands and the same cancers, and anyone who dared to stop and think about it could only wonder why the medical profession had ever split into one order for a beast and another for all remaining beasts in the first place.

Dr Lunette had grown up in the old newsagent's, where the farmers came to stock up on Maas tobacco and hung around for hours afterwards, confident that the beets in their fields would not stop growing in the meantime. In summer, when the door was open and the sheepdogs were snapping irritably at flies, the cigarette mist wafted out, carrying ever louder and more drunken voices with it. The seeds for many of the painful diagnoses Dr Lunette would later make were laid before her eyes in her father's shop. It was largely in that small shop that Gilbert Dock's moustache gradually yellowed from the smouldering stubs he left dangling until the heat on his blistered lip forced him to spit out what was left of the roll-up and immediately use his tongue to slobber another paper shut.

Listening in as a child between the newspapers and the racks of tobacco to all those stories of the ups and, especially, the downs of the various herds and flocks must have inspired Dr Lunette's choice of what to study, and she earned her place in the annals of the village by becoming the first local female with a university degree to stick in a pretty frame. Her ability to rattle off the Latin names of all kinds of phalanges and obscure muscles was taken as definitive proof of her intelligence and, from then on, everyone felt confident to consult her for their own health and well-being. Because when it came to their animals, people around here rarely or never felt the need for medical advice: they rolled up their own sleeves to turn a calf; they needed no assistance to pour disinfectant into a sheep's annually festering arse; and many a man could tell you that a cow with an incurable disease had given him a grateful and somehow loving look when he rested his double-barrel between her two immense eyes. All things considered, Dr Lunette could count herself lucky that she was able to lay her stethoscope now and then on chests that were more than hairy enough for her to maintain her professional pride as a veterinarian, otherwise she would have been forced to go elsewhere to earn a living.

If elderly women were occasionally reluctant to unbutton their pinafores before Dr Lunette's critical eye, this had less to do with the injured vanity a director might ask his actors to express when their character is being palpated by a vet, than with a certain embarrassment due to their still seeing this doctor as the newsagent's little girl, an old acquaintance who was suddenly requesting intimacy with your insides, enquiring about the colour of your stools and asking questions men feared when the years commanded their prostates to falter. The child you had once thrashed for climbing up to your ripest apples could now read the tidings of your body; she was the kind of person who didn't need a first name. The oldest regretted the decline of the custom of wearing hats, because what did today's youngsters have left to take off their heads when they bumped into the doctor on the street?

*

Setting off down the hill to hear his death sentence from her lips, Monsieur Potter had not considered himself any less bestial than anyone else, neither did he doubt Dr Lunette's abilities. But the prospect of ever meeting this woman outside her professional capacity, by bumping into her on the street, for instance, and having to carry out a polite conversation with her was something he had considered anything but desirable. She was a hearty battle-axe, with a hairdo that expressed an aversion to frivolity and heavy glasses that had left a deep, rosy welt on the bridge of her nose. When taking a patient's blood pressure, she tended to grab them in a kind of headlock, as if anticipating a bite, and when she pulled on her rubber gloves the victim would suddenly shrink, knowing that she had just recently been in a cow up to her shoulder and had been known to describe in detail how much she loved the feel of that moist, visceral warmth.

Every time they had adopted another stray dog, Monsieur Potter and Madame Verona had taken it down the hill to see how much its journey had debilitated it, discover its age, get it dewormed if it was young and, very occasionally, find out who its previous owners had been. And every time Dr Lunette had adopted a condescending attitude to this couple who took the fate of these ridiculous pariahs to heart. She condemned the sentimentality, the charity, what she saw as the misplaced empathy of human for animal. 'Why are you giving this mongrel a home? You don't know where it's been, it could be dangerous. Someone chased it off and they must have had a reason.

Have some kids if you feel such a compulsion to be affectionate!' Try explaining to her that she had the terminology wrong, that it wasn't so much a question of their giving a dog a home as a dog having chosen them. Was this the kind of place where a child would dare to let a tear fall on the table where their cat had just had death injected into its veins?

Science had made Dr Lunette laconic and insensitive to the anxieties her tormented patients sweated out on her table. Moreover it was only the strong of character who managed to get in and out of her surgery in less than two hours. Dr Lunette's compulsive yacking was feared more than her rough manner; anyone who had been examined by her knew every illness in the village. She raged about the drunks and the smokers, she raged about those who fried their sausages in large quantities of butter, she called them by name and provided the dimensions of their livers in the hope of their serving as a negative example. No one knew whether veterinarians also took the Hippocratic oath – horses and goats might not mind indiscretion – but it meant that there was no point in even thinking about having a pregnancy terminated in this village without someone else finding out about it that very same day.

The only thing Monsieur Potter had really considered while sitting between the skeletons in her waiting room was his hypochondriac tendency. But the pain that had floated between kidney and lung for weeks on end and whose location he, to Dr Lunette's immense displeasure, was unable to specify to the exact millimetre was, in combination with his nocturnal coughing fits and the threads of blood he found in his saliva every morning, difficult to brush off as a symbol. And since he was, after all, a smoker, she gave her diagnosis without any trace of pity – *only yourself to blame* – and he accepted it immediately. He had no desire to wait for the immaculate white of a hospital room where he would rot away until the ECG plateaued and a beeping machine called the hospital corpse washers to attention and got them sopping their sponges.

We know that he set himself the task of amassing as much firewood as possible for his beloved, warmth he had wanted to give her with his arms. When he had finally finished, he dished up one last serving of love and, God, was he imagining it, Madame Verona swallowed him from below and seemed unwilling to release his penis, even when it had actually grown too limp for her muscles to grip, as if she realized what he had kept secret and wanted to prolong the embrace. That afternoon he withdrew into the wood – *I could die here* – and hanged himself from a tree whose name he could, by then, easily have revealed to us.

VII

If there was one thing wrong with Oucwègne it was the peculiar fact that the previous generation had propagated itself almost exclusively in sons, a plague which, strangely enough, tends to strike remote and sparsely populated regions. There *was* the benevolence of Lucy, the only girl in the afflicted generation, but by herself even Lucy couldn't prevent Oucwègne from gradually emptying. When the morale of those who were left began to flag and the need for relief became overwhelming, Tosh would organize an excursion to a nearby city where the prostitutes were theirs for the choosing. Nights in which they were able to wear themselves out, full of women who would hopefully help them to get a load off their minds as well.

Not everyone looked forward to losing himself in the strumpets of La Neptune because shattering romantic illusions didn't come cheap, and, second, it had happened more than once that they had headed off in the minibus singing like a bunch of schoolboys only to drive back from the girls in a mood of deadly dejection. Later, on the bank of the river, the fool's paradise they were returning from would be good for the requisite tall stories, sprayed cheerfully out of mouths full of sausage or fish, but at the moment itself every one of them had been pushed back into his own cellar. A guy like Alfredo was always so intimidated by the shamelessness of the nymphaeum that he had to drown his fears so thoroughly that when he reached the point at which he could finally relax he was always too pissed to get it up.

*

The reason why hardly any girls had been born here in the last few decades could possibly be explained with complicated diagrams with arrows leading from one DNA structure to another, supplemented by tables of menstrual cycles, but people in Oucwègne had already reconciled themselves to the theory that the depraved seed of drunkards loses the power to produce a thing of beauty. This was a reference to the days in which the north was still destitute and its men descended to these parts to register as seasonal labourers. They let themselves be quartered in barracks and helped harvest the sugar beets. Boys with unblemished faces and trouser pockets worn out from unemployment and boredom.

Many of them had left the area of their birth for the first time, many had never dirtied their hands before. At home mothers and, in some cases, wives waited for their wages and letters. But few among them could write and their pride prevented them from dictating the details of their homesickness to someone who could handle a pen. Plus: they had already drunk their wages, as inexhaustible as they had seemed to youths accustomed to keeping their money in a sock.

And the local girls – eyeing and ogling and gig-gling and carolling the northerners' looks to each other (photos are all that's left of them now, but in those photos they remain young for ever and bursting out of their clothes) – took the step from virginity to motherhood in one much too fleeting entanglement. Nothing could have been further than fatherhood from most of the fathers' thoughts: as soon as the dung carts returned to the beet fields, the handsome northerners headed home, no doubt after making false promises to ensure that, instead of soothing an angry mob, the stationmaster could watch the snot-wet hankies flap when his whistle set the train in motion. The sons who were born of deceit months later bore their mothers' names, their rotten roots kept secret from church and town hall. Since then a curse has hung over the area's wombs and, apart from a few exceptions, only boys have been dangled over the baptismal font.

*

The dangers of celibacy are familiar from ecclesiastical circles, and the fear of psychological damage gave some of the area's young men the courage to pack their bags and try their charms elsewhere. In the cases of Dominique and Vincent, even with success. Enjoying the privilege of snuggling up against another body had not made them unhappy, not at all, but after a while they realized that chicken never tasted as good as the chicken they remembered. They missed the hooting of the owls, the hills, the tomcats that serviced their harems with noises that failed to clarify whether or not cats enjoyed satisfying their urges, the singing in the canteen of the Catholic cinema, the grilled sausages in the summer under a ceiling of stars… and the homemade wine. They wanted to show their rapidly growing sons how to skip stones in the river of their own childhood, and argued the case with their wives day and night until they wore them down and got them to consent to going to live in that remote hole where lies about your age are unmasked by the hill. And where the climb turned their bottoms into real hams.

*

Damien was less lucky: he remained fatalistically smitten with Lucy – lonely Lucy, a saint in some ways, the queen of the back seat, the rustle in the shrub – and had no choice but to wait until she grew too old to render emergency assistance. Rolling in it, poor Damien. The pruning of his family tree and the resulting inheritances had been more than enough to make him the area's biggest landowner by the age of twenty. Parents looking to farm their daughters out to someone who had it made would have been only too willing to sniff up the smell of the manure that hung in clods from his bones, but an angel had blown the horn of penance at the foot of every bed: daughters were simply not conceived, no matter what tricks and positions people used to this end during their lovemaking. Lucy remained an exception, as if Mother Nature had whipped her up in between times to keep her hand in, before returning to her cruel male-only production line.

*

In the stories they read as children in Sister Zoe's class, boats were rarely boats. They were canoes – no, they were schooners, and they took the protagonists straight to the shores of paradise. But these books never evoked a longing for other places, not in Damien, not in Alfredo, not in Mazza and not in Thibaud; all of the local bachelors seemed immune. They owned the fastest cars and the paintwork was always buffed up like new, but none of them had the slightest intention of setting out on a legendary drive. This was the place where they were almost completely happy; anyone who plays for high stakes knows that most people would rather not tempt fate. They accepted the lack of women. Not gladly, but they accepted it. All things considered, the wound caused by the birth statistics was nowhere near fatal and you never – this was a law! – *looked* for a woman. You found her. So they stayed here, on the banks of the Gemontfoux, where there were verses left to sing and more beer to drink. And see how their chances had taken a turn for the best: Madame Verona had been widowed and she had stayed here all the same.

As if the north had sent an emissary to settle its debts.

VIII

When the abandoned were still lovers, they had sworn that they didn't want to live without each other, they had given each other power of attorney over the meaning of their existence and the disappearance of one would have cried out for the disappearance of the other. With the elderly that is often a natural process: if one drops dead, the other hurries to the grave without any extra effort on their part. But young adults are not yet capable of dying like swans; their hearts are able to bear grief and they are forced to resort to the kind of methods that can be found in such beautiful examples in the works of William Shakespeare. Of course Madame Verona had once told her husband that she would follow him into what she imagined, possibly erroneously, as endless darkness, taking the oath that many lovers had taken before her, and anyone who feels compelled to question their sincerity at such a time has only their own failures to blame.

Was it the smell of meat that set a dog to barking at the marble in the cemetery on the day that Monsieur Potter's last resting place was being fathomed, or had it been drawn there by something else? Madame Verona watched them slide the slab over her sweetheart's grave and walked alone, something she would do on many occasions to come, across the windy hilltop marked with the names of the dead. Names that were linked to the inconsequential history of this village and no longer stirred anyone's lips. Her dead sweetheart had now been entered in the village necrologies under his real name, his northern name, the name that government departments used to write to him and no one here knew.

The villagers had given him the name Potter after hearing that he was an artist and concluding that he must be a potter, perhaps because people here preferred the utility of jugs and vases to the significance of sarabands and sonnets. Not that he was embraced any less gently when it dawned on them that he was a composer, not at all, but the name Potter stuck as an endearment. When Madame Verona finally descended the cemetery path, the dog stopped barking at the marble, followed her, and kept following her. Awaiting it that evening was an enormous meal, as she couldn't get used to cooking for just herself, and a blanket it could mark with its scent. And so, before she knew it, Madame Verona had been drawn into living on for her allotted span.

*

People had expected to see a removals van negotiating the difficult road up the hill, with Madame

Verona returning to a place from her past where she had a thread to pick up, the kind of crossroads everyone passes through several times in their lifetime, where she would now try another turning. After all, everyone had assumed that moving to the remote village of Oucwègne had been Monsieur Potter's idea. It was common knowledge that artists turned their backs on civilization in order to create it; they were hermits, they sliced off their ears or distilled their colours from the Pacific. Poets wrapped their words in clouds, they spoke in mists like nebulists who dipped their brushes in the thickest of fogs, and composers, God yes, composers, they couldn't be all there either.

It was Jean-Paul, by the way – Jean-Paul who bought horses' tails from the farmers to string his bow, and played the sacristan's tunes on his fiddle in church – who drew his friends' attention to the similarity between Monsieur Potter and other, more famous composers. And he named Ravel, the great Maurice Ravel, who had managed to think up a melody that was happy to be whistled by bricklayers, hairdressers, office clerks, managing directors and nursery school teachers, more than once lightening the waiting for incorrigibly late girl- or boyfriends. He too had left the city, in his case Paris, to relocate to a virtually inaccessible hill in Monfort-l'Amaury. The gradient was such that more than once Ravel went tumbling through his garden like a circus acrobat and the movers lugging his things up the hill swore under their breath and cursed his piano as far less than grand. He too had created an illusion of isolation around his staves in the hope of writing his pièce de résistance, an ambition which, as we now know, was realized. All in all, more than enough reason to assume it had not been Madame Verona who had insisted on moving here.

When asked about the nature of his work, Monsieur Potter summed up a few classics – Bach's cello suites, a Barber adagio, Pergolesi's *Stabat Mater* – and explained that a particular kind of algebraic operation applied to these three well-known pieces would come up with what he composed, at least as far as the mood was concerned. Melancholy music that made pot plants grow, and Jean-Paul was not alone in reaching this conclusion. One of the village's rougher characters was Tosh, who purchased a symphonic work now and then and even enjoyed the attention when others playfully ridiculed him because of it. But the one who could tell us the most about Monsieur Potter's work was Charlo, a twenty-stone colossus, a mass of fat and friendliness, insatiable at the table, with hands that reminded art historians of the oeuvre of Permeke. A man who strode between his pigs with a holster on his hip and kept their predestined path to the meat hook short and painless. True in his love for the songs of Daniel Balavoine.

Unless he had absolutely set his mind on it, he was impossible to get drunk, but once in that pleasant zone that precedes drunkenness – a zone which, unfortunately, so many people pass through so quickly – an enormous grin that pushed the flesh of his massive jaws up towards his ears would appear on his face and he would start singing. Or else he whistled the kind of tunes that can be expected from people who have served out a large part of their lives surrounded by birds. Monsieur Potter loved those tunes, and even visited Charlo at home now and then to write them down. But a sober Charlo was incapable of producing anything even slightly noteworthy. That was why people sometimes saw Monsieur Potter leaving his hill with three bottles of whisky and several sheets of lined music paper, headed for Charlo, the most scientific approach since Bartók visited the gypsies with blank scores and writing materials. Once the third bottle had been broached, a whole aviary came bursting out of Charlo, who twittered away while on the other side of the table Monsieur Potter drew lines and black circles at a furious rate, like a stenographer for blackbirds and finches. Several of those tunes were effectively repeated in Monsieur Potter's oeuvre, but Charlo never dared to attend one of the performances, largely because his wardrobe did not and would never include anything that would allow him, so he thought, unproblematic admission to a concert theatre.

*

But it was no longer necessary. The composer was dead, and his widow had stayed on her hill. The latter gave Oucwègne strength. Because if the far-too-premature widows in stories have always been lifted straight from creation's showroom, Madame Verona was no exception. We'll go easy on the paper and ink and limit ourselves to the red hair that hung down to her shoulders in spiralling ringlets; her eggshell complexion; her sunny eyes fixed at eternal noon; her slenderness and suppleness; the smile that set everything free, as pure as mathematics, and capable of inflicting a temporary paralysis on the more sensitive; the unreasonable legs that pedestalled all this; and every curve imaginable to go with it. A body that had been given to someone who no longer existed and was now possessed by a void she loved. A waste of natural resources, whichever way you looked at it. Here she would stay, and her beauty would frump away from the sausages she scoffed with everyone else on the banks of the Gemontfoux. She stayed, knowing that the hill would later become her Calvary and finally her harsh contract with loneliness. You had to hand it to her, for someone from the north. And the day this news passed through these hills – Madame Verona is staying! Madame Verona's staying! – the men sang while pissing globs of froth into the river.

IX

When the ewes could finally lick what they had yeaned with such difficulty, the quarrymen had coughed the slate dust that piled ever higher in their lungs out into the sink, the thermoses had been rinsed, the horseshoes hammered, the fields sown, the hay raked and tedded, the concrete poured, the cords of wood delivered and the money counted – in short, when the work was done and the time had come to forget that tomorrow would be another day of yeaning and coughing and rinsing and hammering and that they would once again have to sow and rake and ted, pour and deliver in order to hopefully end up with something left to count – then, and only then, would the men head for the canteen of the old Catholic cinema for their nightcaps. And because sleep always comes sweeter after a victory, any kind of victory, they split into pairs that battled each other over the table-football table, playing a game that could not possibly be seen as a surrogate version of football, but was a completely different thing, which they judged to be, in both importance and difficulty, far superior to the supposed original.

In utmost concentration they stooped over the playing field, channelling all the strength of their shoulders and arms into their wrists so that, with a bang that was loud but dry, they could send the wooden ball rocketing to the other end, and prefer- ably straight into the goal. They sweated over neat dribbles, feints and crosses, forcing openings in the field and getting so carried away they forgot how ter- ribly unhappy they were without beer and cigarettes. Worse still: anyone who dared interrupt play for a quick slug or a comforting drag on a smouldering fag was in for dirty looks; he had disrupted the rhythm of the game, disturbing their concentration. Curses and cries of joy held each other in check, blunders were made good with looks of intense self-contempt.

It was supremely serious, it was war and, as is well known, war is much too serious a business to be left to soldiers and statesmen. At the same time, a game of table football was a much better opportunity to taste the pleasures men traditionally derive from bloodbaths. The little ball bounced and rattled, clack, tack; the miniature wooden players, painted red and blue, spun on their steel rods; you heard the screws screaming for a drop of oil, and only when a liberating 'olé' had burst from two throats and the scoreboard had been adjusted with sadistic precision was a brief silence allowed to descend over the table for the time it took to wipe a face dry with a handkerchief before the ball was put into play again, backs bent, handles gripped tight, and the sounds of battle resumed. The dreams of the approaching night promised to be the most beautiful when the opposing team had been brushed aside with a bagel; then the winners would hoist the table up off the ground so that the losers could crawl under it in the eyes of all present, as if it were a victory arch. A high-spirited humiliation. Afterwards they dunked their sweaty mugs in the canteen's washing-up tub or distracted attention away from their steaming armpits by using a spray meant for disguising unwholesome toilet smells. The hatchet was always buried on the losers: they paid for the next round and took the liberty of summoning up gout, hernias or other bodily ailments as legitimate excuses for their substandard performance.

*

Monsieur Potter had been able to maintain his honour during these matches, perhaps because he had spent part of his childhood at a boarding school where the priests tried to alleviate their pupils' imprisonment by providing them with an hour's recreation every evening in a room where table football and table tennis made an almost unbearable racket. He had retained some degree of skill and understanding of the game as possibly the only lasting benefit of his years of boarding school – besides his deep loathing of religion – but nowhere near enough to rank him among the better players of Oucwègne. He cherished his victories – he did have them – all the more and the childish pleasure that could be plucked from them had a longer use-by date for him than for the others, who always imagined themselves as good as their last game. The imaginary victory rosettes pinned to their chests wilted the moment their vengeful opponents spat into their hands and confidently slipped a coin into the slot.

Women did not play. That, at least, was the general opinion, and the chroniclers of this village must admit that there were indeed few ladies who armoured themselves in bluff and tried their luck at table football. Whenever Monsieur Potter and

Madame Verona challenged another duo, they noticed how difficult it was to get anyone to play against. The others found it hard to raise the enthusiasm, simply because there was no honour to be had from defeating a woman. Instead of playing *against* a woman, they would rather have played *with* a woman. Because someone who could win with a woman by his side really *was* good. He could have just as easily floored the other team by himself, that was the idea behind it, and that was how people took it. In this game, being a good partner was one thing; being a good opponent was a much bigger thing.

*

Of course the men were delighted to see that, as a widow, Madame Verona still regularly came down the hill to visit the canteen of the old cinema, where one mastered the past by forgetting it, and stories told in her presence cautiously detoured around Monsieur Potter until she was hardened in her pain. As if he had never existed, as if no one could believe that it would do her good to hear people talk about him again. Maybe that was why she was never asked to join a game: people were used to seeing her play alongside Monsieur Potter, their inseparability (unhealthy in the eyes of some) manifesting itself in this too. The assumption was that she would not want any memories of table football beyond those she had accumulated with her husband. What's more, people remembered her taking defeat in her stride, even though the urge to win was the first and most important rule.

The players noticed her cheers and accepted her sharing in the delights and despairs of their games, but never thought of inviting her to join in a duel. Until the day she tossed a coin onto the table, wrapped her hands confidently around the grips on the rods, and said, 'OK, who's brave enough?' They could have taken her gestures as a parody of their own masculinity, and it is quite possible that it was only their self-respect that drove them to other interpretations. Such as: with this gesture Madame

Verona was casting aside her grief, she was ready for a new life. Of course, nobody got a new life, that was just a figure of speech. After all, life wasn't like a story being written in a notebook – you couldn't draw a line under it and carry on with a completely different story in the same notebook. But people liked to resort to that illusion when faithfulness to a memory was making it hard to find the courage to live on. Starting over again, dividing everything up into chapters because you can end them, and constantly telling yourself how easy it is.

That was human nature and that was how humans arranged their history. They drew a line under organized genocide and started a new story with room for laughter, poetry and advertisements for underwear. So that it would seem as if it were humans themselves who were rejecting and reinventing mankind, over and over, as if they had nothing to do with their own past. That was why people found it so easy to make paintings of gruesome battles that had once taken place and find them picturesque.

That was why all genocides will one day become paintings that will be praised for their coloration. And that was why, or so they must have thought for a moment at the table-football table, Madame Verona had begun a new life. Because she could not possibly let herself be loved by another unless the life she had shared with Monsieur Potter had been a different life. Only a new life could let her believe that the old one had died with her lover. This was the only way that young widows could give their bodies without guilt, without feeling adulterous. Because where there's life there's lust.

And yes, suddenly the men wanted to play table football with her. No doubt about that. With her and against her. And her being scared of winning was irrelevant. Because they too were willing to end chapters, even unfinished ones, to start one in which a woman would play a more prominent role.

X

Spurred on by the effects of a bottle of pastis under the plane tree, the bachelors imagined what it would be like to be allowed to make love to Madame Verona. And although their heroic impulses were not completely crushed by the power of their imaginations, they concluded, each for themselves, that they would come back down to the valley after The Great Event as a loser. They could already picture themselves en route, calm yet hesitant, presumably to prolong the beauty that can be found in melancholy, hands in pockets, drowsy, the way you should be after proper lovemaking. But in none of their fantasies was one of them permitted to sleep off his languor in her arms. Because only in sleep are people truly honest. That was when they gave off unsavoury odours, grunted, passed wind and dreamed out loud. Madame Verona would never give that much of herself to anyone again. And so they had to leave the bed, gathering up their clothes and pulling them on, telling her they understood. With wounded pride: 'I understand.' And adding: 'Don't get up, I'll close the door behind me,' before vacillating over a kiss they don't give or give only half-heartedly, symbolically, in the air. 'I'm sorry,' she would say, not to her lover, not even to herself, but to the young man in the photo beside her bed. She would spend the night alone surrounded by the awkward smell of coitus, possibly because one way or the other she had learned in the meantime to appreciate solitude. And because she wanted to cry her heart out. Striding down the hill, the lover would be in no doubt on that score: he was leaving someone behind in tears. Real tears, like the ones shed at the dawn of humanity, when you could harvest salt from girls' cheeks.

Some of them thought that even this fantasy was pushing things and considered the bedroom overly audacious, a place that was tied to her amorous past like no other. Monsieur Potter had undoubtedly left an imprint of his body on the mattress, a hollow she rolled into gently in the evenings, fitting into him, contained in his absolute embrace. There could be no question of her choosing that location when, as a widow, for the first time, she... And they swallowed the words. Not from embarrassment, but to savour them. No, it was cold hard floors you should be thinking. In the most merciful instance, they would try the sofa first, but awkward positions and fumbling and sudden thoughts of towels to considerately avoid leaving any stains would spoil the fun.

*

Of course the man would come first. Too soon, what's more, before he had come close to losing himself in the depths of the rhythm they had found together. But he kept his end up, believing in inexhaustible Negroes who had left their traces in his white man's blood, invoking them, worshipping them, and not for a second thinking that as far as she was concerned he could have suspended his efforts long ago, and the war of attrition he provided as a courtesy came over as nothing more and nothing less than a display of masculine pride.

*

We enter their fantasies, they don't mind, and we see her lying there. On her back. She is naked, completely, because she cannot bear the playfulness of making love with garments left on here and there. That was the old days, sometimes. Here, her nakedness serves to avoid exposing herself more than is necessary, but she alone knows that. She endures it, but her endurance is no submission. Her hands are in his hair, she *has* to put them somewhere. And although that image is open to many interpretations, we feel moved to think that she is doing it to steer him, or rather, restrain him, for instance, when she feels his head descending. Not that. And him understanding: not yet. Because he is building up credit, showing understanding and patience, and his head slides back up.

If we look at those hands in that hair, we notice a finger with a band of paler flesh, the place she wore her ring – *the* ring, because real rings do not tolerate indefinite articles – which she has now removed. Some women shed their rings before committing adultery, no matter how convinced they might be, and Madame Verona was definitely one of them. Symbols depend on the animistic philosophies of their inventors and in that regard wedding rings have it easy. Madame Verona has laid hers on the cupboard, and knows that even a glance in that direction will make her burst into uncontrolled weeping. And she *will* weep. But not now. This evening. Tonight. Lying in her imprint, alone. So she looks up. At the ceiling, we might think, but we would be miscalculating. She's looking right through the ceiling. And if she closes her eyes for a moment, he will think: she likes what I'm doing now, I have to keep this up. He concentrates on a movement, a spot. She thinks: his hands act but don't feel. If she could reach a clinical orgasm, she would have made an effort in that direction, not from desire, but from hunger, a chemical need, but finally she asks him to stop. I'm OK like this; We shouldn't have even started; Let's pretend it never happened.

There shouldn't be a moon in the sky, neither half nor full, and no rain should fall with misleading appropriateness when the lover walks down the hill. There shouldn't be anything, neither day nor night, and he will know that in that instant she is showering. That humiliation, at least, has been spared him. He didn't stay the night, he didn't have to see her creep out of bed, didn't have to listen to the water gurgling in an adjoining room. Because she was scrubbing herself with her sponge to expunge him. Few men can bear a woman who slips into the shower immediately after an embrace, and he was not one of them. Wet and new, she would have lain down beside him with her back unbridgeable inches away and not a trace of their union perceptible on her skin. All overwhelmed by fresh-spring or cool-ocean or however the soap perfume was misleadingly described on the box. The only delight he gave was to one of her dogs, the umpteenth hunting dog, which sat up at the sound of a man coming down the stairs, watched him leave the house solitary in heart and number, and was overjoyed that no one would be staying to compete for a share of her attention.

*

Yes, that was what it would be like, the men knew that almost for a fact, and opening a second bottle of pastis failed to send their thoughts off on another tack. There was no pleasure to be gained from a widow who was doing it for the first time since her bereavement. And they thought it advisable to wait until someone else had taken that thankless task upon himself. They would try their luck later, when Madame Verona had already breached the contract assigning property rights over her body and no longer, or at least less compulsively, thought of Monsieur Potter when a man clove to her mouth. Until that day they would drive their minibus to the young girls of La Neptune, singing and drinking, grasping and grabbing with hands and teeth, and thanking creation for the weakness of the flesh. Unless Lucy let them sing her name and waited in the bushes while they drew straws to decide the order. This was their plan. To be patient – it worked for the trees. Fourteen single men, under the plane tree, under the starry splashes in the black sky, sucking on tobacco-saturated gobs until they were thick enough to spit heroically, deliberating over dreams they tried to hold tight after they had said goodbye and were climbing the hills to their homes.

And no one there to paint them.

XI

Returning to that cold February day, we see that Madame Verona is still down in the valley, sitting on a bench the council has placed there for the benefit of exhausted walkers; the dog lying at her feet in blind trust. She knows that she won't re-ascend, that she has reached the point at which she exists only as past. It is quite possible that her body would allow her to keep going for a few more years – she is counting on strength of will to die today. Snow has started to paint the world white, an exercise in disappearing. Because she will never see any of the things that submit to that covering of white again.

She has never liked looking at things the way you are supposed to look at them for the last time: a town where you have spent a pleasant holiday, now slowly shrinking in a rear-view mirror; a train racing from stripe to spot; the head of a lover leaning out of a window of that train… But now she seems to enjoy it, that kind of looking, perhaps because she herself is already part of that disappearing, who can say? She breathes in the smell of the snow, enough to take a Proust back eighty years, when snow smelled just the same and she dissected that smell for the first time, moulding it into a tiny morsel and curiously popping it into her mouth to let it slowly melt.

But it is her fingers that capture our attention in this scene. She taps the arm of the bench. Drumming her fingers. From impatience, we might decide, and no one could hold our conclusion against us. Or to ease the cold. Even if she's not afraid of the death from exposure the coming night will grant her. After all, she has heard enough stories about reckless mountaineers who started turning blue mid-climb, went delirious and died with a face that was twisted with delight. Looking at those fingers, we notice a peculiar interplay with her feet. As if she's operating the pedal of an invisible sewing machine. There is also a certain structure to the way she's tapping her fingers.

Of course, she's playing the piano, it's obvious. A merry, simple tune she taught to countless children at the music school, because that was what she did for all those years: spending hours on a piano stool with fledgling little people, semi-talented at best, the wildest hope being that they might one day be up to playing a ragged boston or a drunken waltz at a birthday party, more than satisfied with the predictable remark of one of the guests: 'I didn't know you could play the piano! And so well!' Madame Verona had seen more than enough of them, teenage girls who slid their knees in under the piano in a way that showed immediately just how tedious they found her lessons to be.

The boys signed up when they had failed to make the grade in a sport that might have given them some kind of status, girls fell for the dresses they had seen lady pianists wearing on TV – glamour they considered essential to the sound. Or else they were mummy's girls, who dreamed of putting on an impressive, almost perfect Christmas Eve perform-ance of *Silent Night* while flanked at the piano by a grandfather to the left and an aunt to the right, this after the brat had presented her astonishing exam results to the entire family and just before she needed restraining to prevent her from demonstrating her progress as a ballerina. Madame Verona saw the youngsters cooling their dance fury in discotheques where the tarted-up melodies blared out of machines that gradually eroded their musical taste buds, that was her firm conviction, and it would have left her cold if someone had cautiously pointed out that her ideas were buoyed up by conservatism or senescence.

Her students had raged against solfège, invoking rock singers who couldn't tell a *re* from a *si* but had still reaped success and in whose footsteps they hoped to follow. They thought scales were pointless and used the swear words that happened to be in at the time to reject the methods of renowned music teachers. She had seen enough of it as a child progressing year after year to ever-smaller classes; the concept of discipline had been contaminated under the regime of a madman with followers, no one seemed to grasp that an instrument required the very thing that had once been used to hurry the world to an orderly apocalypse. Her efforts yielded, very rarely, an adult who regretted having given up music much too young.

*

Madame Verona knew that her colleagues saw her as *the wife of.* The wife of the composer who was esteemed by some and reviled by others, the way it goes. The longer she taught, the less she felt at home in the world where she had once met her husband. Her: just outgrown childhood, shy, the girl who strode through her days weighed down by her cello. Him: smoking impatiently outside the rehearsal room, the promising young pianist with the dandy-ish shirt and neglected fingernails. The year before he left to study composition at the conservatoire.

Until that day they were extras in each other's lives, passers-by in a long corridor. Now they were to play together, an exercise, a siciliano by Fauré, and they would never forget it. The result was pathetic, her hands gleamed with perspiration and skidded on the strings, the teacher used the word desecration. But later that same month they consecrated the city's parks, and their arms too were sacred as they held each other while falling in love, and she listened to the encyclopaedic knowledge which young men are so anxious to pass on to their girlfriends. In no time the young couple were referred to in sly asides as 'Jacqueline and Daniel', after a cellist and a pianist who were torn apart so tragically that it was only a matter of time before their lives were filmed. Ah, the days when they were only just budding, all the things that would have at most until this freezing night to come to fruition.

And suddenly she was there at the conservatoire herself, as a teacher. Piano of all things, his instrument. In the staff room during the breaks her colleagues subjected her to small talk about handbags, TV shows, recipes, the advantages and disadvantages of the latest coffee machine, where to go for risotto and which wine one should drink with sashimied fish fillet. Yawn. Conversations Madame Verona avoided with economical nods. On your birthday you brought in chocolates, a staff-room tradition that confronted her every year with the fact that she had forgotten her own birthday yet again, leading others to conclude she was going downhill. *What are you doing up there in that forest? You'll never meet anyone that way. Come back to civilization. Get yourself a bloke. Life goes on...* They meant well, if nothing else.

*

The song she was tapping out on the bench in her last hours was one that Monsieur Potter had written at her request, searching for a melody that would make children enjoy playing the piano. She played it often herself, in her sleep, with her fingers on the sheets. More than once she had caught herself tapping it out on the steering wheel at a red light. It wasn't something she thought about, the tune was in her fingers, in her fingers and in her feet, so that once, daydreaming, she had even driven into the middle of an intersection, forgetting that it was an accelerator she was pressing. She considered this a missed opportunity and by far the most beautiful way she'd had of coming closer to – how can you keep finding soothing names for it? The lowering bowers? – driving to her death while imagining she was playing that tune.

But we would be mistaken to think that, on this February day, Madame Verona was going to let a corresponding opportunity pass her by, daydreaming on a bench, her head a music box that would never close again. It was what she wanted, there was no doubt about that, but she had underestimated the cold and preferred her reunion with the void to be painless. She stood up. Just to stretch her legs for a moment, that was all; her mind was made up. The dog shook the snowflakes from his coat, wagging his tail, glad of a new distraction. 'There's no bone, boy, where you're following me.' But that didn't seem to bother him. 'We should actually find a good home for you first.' She had wanted to go out like a light, calmly and without any fuss. And now she realized that simply dying is bloody hard work and that an awful lot would be asked of her before this snow had melted, the rivers surged like spring and the early lambs were unwittingly bleating eternal life.

XII

Everyone would remember that it happened the year a cow became mayor of Oucwègne. A cow, that's right – more precisely, a Blonde d'Aquitaine, known by farmers as an exceptional beef breed. Her phenomenal rump made her the queen of the annual fairs, her coat of soft-pile carpet had a colour that went well with most furniture, even modern, and when she mooed it was never from discontent but always an apt comment from the sidelines, witty and pertinent. There was hardly a farmer to be found who would prod and hit his Blonde d'Aquitaine to get her into a truck. She was not an animal – come now – but some beauty who, after an adventure with the gods, had assumed the form of a cow. The ancient Greeks had animalized people left, right and centre and their foolishness was still taught today without a trace of irony. And although these sentiments are chiefly attributed to children who refuse to plunge their fork into the rabbit they patted the day before, many a farmer found it simply impossible to bite into his own Blonde d'Aquitaine. A Blonde d'Aquitaine in a field in a valley, that was a happy marriage of body and soil.

*

OK, there was a mayor of course, a real one, with a salary and royal recognition, who showed his face at festivities and bought round after round when elections were due, a man of copious flesh and viscous blood, fattened up on working lunches and bloated from boozing at receptions, obliged to take care of road signs and parking fines, the naming of streets and the enforcement of building zones. His was the signature on hunting permits and fishing licences, the representative of the law, the ostentatious laughter after every joke, the sympathetic nod after every sentence. No one had anything *personal* against the man, but his life took place between piles of papers, his office was a long way away behind the hills, in the city, where he made decisions about seven other communities as well.

What's more, he was a member of a political party, which didn't mean much here because whether the sash was hung over a Catholic, a socialist, a liberal or something else, the sun shone just as long. But here too people had suffered through a war with good guys and bad guys, and afterwards they had thought it more sensible to call a taboo down on political convictions. They had felt the need for a mayor of their own, one who didn't need to divvy his promises out over eight communities, who steered clear of red tape, and whose public burps and farts could never cause offence. Someone without a flag, that was it. Someone they would appoint for just one task: plunging Oucwègne into entertainment for the duration of his term of office. Celebrations, that was what the mayor was there for, to come up with celebrations and games and nothing else. And since those who make their living off the land are acquainted with fortune's daily tombola, they realized that this mayor should not be elected with the means that democracy puts at our disposal, but should be selected by Fate itself: Coincidence. The election was preceded by meetings in which points of view were clarified with flailing arms, and the strength of an argument was determined purely and solely by the volume of its delivery. How to lure Fate all the way to Oucwègne, that was the question.

Finally all present decided that the prospective mayors would need to look for *something* and – after even more palaver – that that *something* might as well be a turnip. They settled on an evening in the beautiful month of July, pitched a tent in the valley and provided so much lubrication that singing would be inevitable later that night. Those who aspired to office were confined in the tent until the turnip had been hidden in fields old Monsieur Canet had made available for that purpose. When the flaps of the tent were pulled back the men hurried out, rash and reckless, sprinting through the streets of Oucwègne to reach the fields, more Elysian than any field had ever been before.

Year after year the men ran through the streets like harried bulls, each obsessed with the idea of finding the turnip. Their haste might have made sense during the first few elections, but several editions later experience had shown that the search could last for days. Not only were Monsieur Canet's pastures extensive, the deep muddy colour of the turnip also made it easy to walk past it without even noticing. It was always half buried, and sometimes the other half was covered with a layer of dung to make sure that pretenders to the throne were kept busy for quite a while parting grass to inspect all the cow pats.

Like much that is infantile, it was highly enjoyable and this system had provided numerous symbolic mayors, each of whom, motivated by pride alone, exerted himself to be the best, the most inventive, the most fun, the most whatever ever. No portraits would ever be painted of these mayors and if the pigeons felt an urge to shit on them, they needed to hurry and aim well, because there weren't going to be any statues to celebrate their glorious policies either. But their immortality was assured, and more genuine too, and after the announcement of each new municipal father the locals danced and boozed until the udders of their cows were about to burst and they all ran off cursing, each to his own milking stool.

*

Everyone would remember that it happened the year a cow became mayor of Oucwègne. The turnip remained hidden for the second night in a row, every turd had been turned over three times already, to no avail. Viking, who was retiring as mayor that year and had had the honour of hiding the vegetable from his aspiring successors, was already being half accused of playing a practical joke – he had the nerve for it – and his repeated assurances that the turnip had been hidden as usual just like every other year were met with despondency. By the morning of the third day it was clear that only Vincent and Damien were able to keep their spirits up for this marathon, and a tense finish seemed in the offing until the turnip was suddenly discovered in the mouth of our Blonde d'Aquitaine.

Statutes were there to be complied with: whosoever found the turnip would be girded with the tricolour sash and had earned the right to call themselves major-domo of Oucwègne for a term of one year. The cow was appointed mayor, there was nothing else for it. The statutes also stipulated that the brand-new mayor would be driven in triumph from the field to the party tent in Benjamin's *deux-chevaux*. Of course, the cow must have thought that her moment had come when they manhandled her into the tiny vehicle. She must have envisaged chopping blocks and blood-smeared butcher's hats. Her future: sliced and wrapped in sheets of red-and-white checked paper. But when she reached the tent and every man jack started kissing her on the mouth, when she heard her owner speaking into a microphone to promise that, given her function, she would not be carted off to the abattoirs, and when she was finally presented with a trough of beer, she grew calmer. Also specified by the statutes: that the incoming and outgoing mayors dance together. Which they did. Viking wasn't much of a one for ballroom dancing, never had been, but the number he performed with the cow demonstrated clear progress in that area. The end of this party is veiled from memory, but there can be no doubt that everyone there, united in friendship, wrapped arms around each other and forgot the death knell.

Blonde d'Aquitaine, the village's first female de facto mayor, grazed her field from that day on with a sash around her bulk. Anyone passing the field greeted her with a friendly 'Good morning, Madame Mairesse,' and on holy days they treated her to garlic bread. But she didn't organize any festivities.

*

Anyway, everyone would remember that it happened when she was made mayor and Charlo was the first to break the news: Madame Verona had been seen with a man. And not just that, Madame Verona had been seen with a man *in her wood*. Furthermore, the man in that wood had worn a suit, Sundayfied from head to toe, the kind of get-up that would have any local immediately rolling with laughter. Whether or not she was holding his hand could not be verified. But soon after, she gave Charlo the job of cutting down the tree her husband had hanged himself from – to the immense joy of the wifeless. Because this was a turning point; a clearer statement could not be imagined. Madame Verona had permanently cast aside her mourning. And if she started something with the besuited gibbon it would simply be a matter of time, waiting until the plates started flying through the living room and then risking a shot yourself. Who would have thought of her deciding to get that highly significant tree chopped down in such a bloody rush?

Cows were harbingers of beauty, it's true. But until that moment their holiness had been known only in India.

XIII

When Rosetta Courthéoux pulled down the shutters in front of her shop for the last time, everyone knew the years of loneliness and isolation had come to stay. She had lowered them slowly, like a flag after the 'Last Post', but anyone attempting to attribute symbolic worth to that slowness was forgetting her age: deteriorating was the only thing she could do at any kind of pace any more, and beyond that Rosetta Courthéoux had completely lost her sense of rhythm. She had been hearing it from all sides for quite a while now ('For goodness' sake,

Rosetta, what are you doing spending all your time in that shop of yours, wouldn't it be better to enjoy the years you have left?'), but no one's queuing up to support a shopkeeper in retirement, and as long as she manned her counter she was assured of her daily chit-chat. She had sold virtually everything there was to sell at some stage of her life and whenever someone requested something she didn't have, she got it in straight away, often in too large a quantity. Everyone remembered how the jars of salted herring had stood there on the shelf unsold for eighteen years. Children came in just to gawp at them, staring goggle-eyed at the processes of biological decay. Hard-to-sell vegetables were left to ferment in their tins for years, sometimes resulting in a rupture that left the stench of, summa summarum, five hundred gallons of liquid manure lingering in the shop for weeks.

But in her eyes nothing was unsellable, a principle that modern sales managers have cribbed from grocers, and she ensured her place in the stories that people never got tired of telling by actually selling her eighteen-year-old herrings – to a Swede with a traditional attachment to feasting on rotten fish. She took it as a matter of pride that not one product she had ever ordered should be removed from her stock. Even when it became obvious that Oucwègne was doomed to die out and the last child to be born in the immediate vicinity had started growing hair in unpleasant places, she still refused to remove the boxes of nappies from her inventory. And lo and behold, that day too arrived when people stood in her shop waiting until the other customers had exchanged their last bits of gossip and left them alone to ask, 'Rosetta, those nappies you used to sell here all those years ago, have you got any of them left in your shed?' The sizes were too small, no doubt about that, but if you pulled a pair of underpants on over the top, those nappies were still good for hiding the first leaks of old age.

★

Rosetta had more faith in her head than in calculators, which she considered too slow and mistrusted as a source of intellectual sluggishness. It took her no time at all to spit out how much the customer had to hand over and if her total was met by incredulous looks from someone who, in department stores, had lost their faith in algebra, she would draw up lightning-fast columns in the margins of old newspapers and do the sums over again out loud as proof. She was no fonder of bank cards, because what good was money you couldn't hold in your hand? If you wanted visible goods, you had to pay with visible money – for her it was that simple.

But since the world had evolved in a direction that required the memorization of a combination of numbers before people could extract their own money from a hole in a wall, and because the nearest money-distributing machine was a good twelve miles away (a trip the elderly undertook less and less frequently, and when they did it was often in vain as the machines were just as likely to be empty), Rosetta

Courthéoux didn't argue about postponing payment. She noted the name of the debtor and the credit extended in exercise books she kept for that purpose. Given her elephantine memory this would have been unnecessary, except for the fact that for the last twenty years of his life Corneille got off with the excuse that the cash machines had run out of money, the bus to town hadn't shown up, his pass had been swallowed... but that he would pay tomorrow, no matter what, and he swore it on his mother's soul and his dog's head. It was never more than bread, a packet of tobacco and a can of beer, and although she knew very well that Corneille would never ever pay his bills, she kept selling him everything on credit. Corneille was a hopeless case, her almost daily excuse for a good deed.

It was an unstoried Tuesday when Corneille stood fidgeting in her shop, letting everyone else jump the queue with the words, 'Go on, I'm in no hurry,' so that Rosetta thought, 'The poor devil, he's reached that stage too, in a minute he'll ask for a box of nappies, promising to come and pay as soon as he can.' But when he was finally left as the last person in the shop, he reached into his back pocket for his wallet, a leather notecase that had moulded itself to the shape of his buttock and almost fell apart like an old Bible, and said, 'Rosetta, you can cross me off in those books of yours, I made it to the bank.'

What surprised her most was that, when going through her exercise books to work out the debt that had accrued over twenty years, she established that Corneille must have had exercise books of his own at home. The amount he laid on her table just before closing time was correct to the last centime. Had Corneille changed his sheets for the first time in all those years and rediscovered his savings? Had an inheritance fallen into his hands, or had he invested the little he had in the national lottery? Or was he one of the many rich people who lead a poverty-stricken life because they're terrified of one day having to buy too many drinks at the pub? These were questions she would never ask him; she was much too polite. But now that the money was lying on her table she realized that Corneille had been her private pension fund. She could close the shop and dawdle along to her last days.

*

It was irreversible, no one suffered any illusions on that score – Oucwègne would speedily join the names of all those other villages that had been sacrificed on the altar of mobility: Bergimont, Charnet, Chersin, Sedrones, Franfays…

Someone had once settled here, a hunter, a fisherman, and when others joined him, they needed to think up a name for the hamlet, because no one ever comes from nowhere, a place that can't be named isn't part of any stories. Someone must have suggested the name Oucwègne and, after tasting the sound of it, the community accepted that name and embraced it. The name would have a future, it would arouse expectations when it appeared on an envelope in a girl's handwriting. Birds didn't need names – every year they returned to their summer residences from the south, and they would keep doing that. But mankind had abandoned this place, drawn to where people become population and the only scenery is cityscape.

Those who stayed, just forty of them, well... they stayed. Unless they had children, because they had seen that tragedy acted out for them by Vincent, intertwined with this village on every side, Monsieur le Président, but one day his children decided he was too old to stay on alone. A giant of a man, big and round, Vincent had a horn in his swollen throat he used to drown out the bullfrogs when the croaking got on his nerves. A man who believed that a diet of five steaks a day would make him immortal, even if he was constantly sucking on the fags he rolled with strong shag. It was, however, his kidneys that gave him trouble and turned him into a stone pisser. 'You don't drink enough!' Dr Lunette told him, adding, 'Water!' to retain some semblance of credibility. He didn't consume *any* water. Water was for cows, which reminded him that Dr Lunette was still an animal doctor. And he would not drink water, not if his life depended on it – he too had his pride. But his children insisted that he move to the city, to one of those homes where white aprons take care of the elderly. Comfort would await him, but he could forget about asking for a second piece of meat. Here he had always been the strongest, the Hercules everyone was only too keen to turn to for help, and it was heartbreaking to see this man – still impressive to look at, but now weak – being put in the car by his children. He cursed them, threatening to die tomorrow to rack their consciences. He drove down the hill spitting, looking at the pale blue winter sky he had always loved and would never see again unless it was through much too clean windows.

And those who stayed, thirty-nine of them now, well… they stayed. With their pétanque balls and their bottles of pastis under the plane tree, and their Aznavour songs that had begun sounding more and more like one potato, two potato, three potato, four.

XIV

'You'll have to forgive me for being so blunt, but your husband would have made my life a lot easier if he'd hanged himself from a spruce.'

*

Yes, that wood. It was the end of the nesting season, the period in which foresters forgot their axes and kept away from their domains. That was the only way the squirrels and birds of prey could work on their dreys and eyries, the only way life could return to the foliage and undergrowth. The trees needed the animals as much as the animals needed the trees. In early July people pulled the laces of their boots tight for the first time since March and stepped timorously into the woods, looking for damage caused by the storms of late spring, beeches that had been blasted by lightning and places where deer had feasted on juicy young shoots. Those who sold their timber on the stump removed sections of bark or used paint and brush to indicate which trunks were on offer.

A lot had changed around here and if you so much as touched upon the subject the local operators would take a cut of tobacco between their fingers and dish up the whole story with sublime swearing. About how timber used to pay. When people still scraped the bowels of the earth to mine coal. They couldn't keep up with the demand, because the companies burrowed deeper and deeper under the ground and the mineshafts needed stronger and stronger shoring with good timber you couldn't plant enough of. Real money, mister, hand over foot, in those days a forest was an earner. But the mines closed down, suddenly, becoming the silent graves of acres and acres of sacrificed woods and Italians who were never found again: young guys, determined to one day return to Lettomanoppello or God knows what they called their particular brand of homesickness, where they would take the most beautiful girl in their arms under the campanile. Buried alive one catastrophic morning. Ah, even those who mourned them have long since passed away.

Coffins, that's what the trees became in the days that followed, coffins for the ones they managed to bring up in bits and pieces. The cheapest kind, from the plainest planks, because the disaster only struck the humble, as the newspapers of the time wrote. But after that, end of story. The pits closed, the pitmen disappeared, and with them the demand for wood. Switching to other kinds of wood, for furniture-making, for instance, wasn't the kind of thing you did overnight. A tree doesn't even catch your eye until it's thirty years old, but if you want to cut a table out of it, you've still got a long wait in front of you.

On top of that, the declaration proper of the war on trees was yet to come, as contradictory as this may sound, when plastic and aluminium suddenly filled the houses. The demand for wood plummeted, the economic value of one of these woods was more or less zilch, and most owners had no choice but to turn to something else to make a living. Not forgetting that meanwhile they had penetrated deep into the Amazonian forests, shamelessly clearing trees that had reached up to the heavens for centuries without human intervention at a rate of dozens of football pitches per hour. Per minute. And paper – that, they recycled. Only fucking morons were left in forestry, that and the odd solipsist here and there, people who had money left under a mattress to invest in the solitude they needed after dissecting mankind so thoroughly that misanthropy was the only possible outcome. Other than that: no one.

Although. Firewood, there were still people in firewood here and there. Firewood and Christmas.

*

Madame Verona accompanied the besuited gentle-
man into the wood thinking of cathedrals. The
comparison was Monsieur Potter's who, when guid-
ing the competition between the dominant trees,
realized that he would never see the fruits of his
labour. Healthy forests need proud old trees – in
a way they're like fathers to the little ones, setting
an example and sharing out the light. Anything
with suckers or wounds needed removing, growing
twisted was punishable by chainsaw. Only straight
trees with harmonious branches and beautiful deep
crowns were selected as trees of the future. Trunk
foragers and their prey prefer them, woodpeckers
would rather ricketick their homes in them, a
forest without giants was as good as dead. But not
a single forest builder had ever lived to have the
enjoyment of the assistance he gave nature. What it
took, and this was no exaggeration, was the spirit of
a cathedral builder: starting something whose completion you would never see. A small adjustment,

even a footstep in the rotting leaves, picking a chanterelle, it changed the course of the next two hundred years. It could have consoled Madame Verona: looking at the trees her husband had spared and seeing how they had quietly started their climb to the sun. And maybe it consoled him too, in the seconds before he jumped, that in a century or two animals would mate and nest in a tree he had put a guard on as a sapling. Foresters are said to generally die peacefully – after all, they made life bigger than themselves.

*

'This is a deciduous tree,' said the man, a *luthier*, because that is the name cello makers much prefer being called. 'You have to realise that cellos are made from conifers. Preferably spruce.' Madame Verona knew very well what cellos were made from, no one needed to lecture her on that score. Norway spruce for the body, felled in the Carpathians at the end of winter, when the flow of sap had come almost to a standstill. Maple for the scroll, ebony for the pegs, Brazil wood for the bow. But her mind was made up, she wanted a cello from the wood of the tree her husband had hanged himself from.

'All right, but if your instrument ends up sounding like a cheese grater, it's on your head.'

And there was *one* other obstacle. Green wood has a mind of its own, sculptors know all about that. They scour shipyards in search of scrapped boats with weary masts. Because wood gives up its fight slowly, even if it's just to carve a beautiful face out of: it would cleave, splinter and crack if it hadn't seasoned a few years first. If a cello was going to be made from this tree, Madame Verona would be wise to summon up the patience to let the wood rest in a dry place for twenty years first.

'In that case I shall live for another twenty years, if I must.'

The cello maker, pardon, the luthier, nodded. The greatest virtuosos had commissioned him; for centuries to come people would be able to listen to the sound of his instruments on all kinds of record-ings, winners of international competitions refused to play cellos that had not been made in his work-shop, and he set his prices accordingly. He had satisfied the most exacting requests, but a cello from a deciduous tree on which a loved one had hanged himself, that was something new. Twenty years. And he rubbed his face, as if to feel how the years had already marked his skin. 'It will end up being my son who makes this cello for you, but by then he'll have mastered the craft better than I ever did, I guarantee you that.'

Two people among the trees, talking about what for the trees was the trifling chasm of oh God oh Lord twenty years.

*

It had been established long in advance that it would be Charlo who would cut down this tree. Simply because you'd have to go a long way to find a better lumberjack. Once, as national champion, he'd won the right to participate in the world wood-chopping championship, and many saw him as *the* man to break the long hegemony of the Canadians and Lapps. Nobody felled a tree with his precision. There where you wanted it, neither an inch to the left nor an inch to the right, that was where his tree would fall. But that year the world title was being fought out in the lion's den, Winnipeg, where the snot hung in stalactites from lumberjacks' noses in the winter, and if there were two things Charlo would never conquer as long as he lived, it was his fear of flying and his mistrust of foreign cooking. His dimensions were those of a healthy birch, a far too overgrown faun whose thighs stretched the largest trousers, with knees creaking from the burden and resoled shoes that never lasted more than a season. The gentlest soul in Oucwègne who, to maintain his equilibrium, cursed a random person for half an hour every day, with the dual purpose of keeping his heart and spirits light while simultaneously exercising his vocabulary. The latter was something that foresters couldn't take for granted – their silences were too long and too frequent, unused as they were to human company. When pretty girls went by they didn't whistle, they rustled. Now he stared at the tree, knowing that Monsieur Potter had hanged himself from it, and asked Madame Verona if she was sure.

He picked up his chainsaw, choked.

*

Silence is often more intense after its return. When a tree accepts its defeat, creaks and capsizes, all life flies up and off. There's crowing and cawing, branches crack, it rains feathers and down, rabbits flee to their underground shelters. All things considered, the titan's contact with the actual ground is quiet; people generally expect it to be louder. It's mainly the rest of the forest that kicks up a fuss and makes a racket. And once the creatures have assessed the damage, silence comes back. Eyes and leaves turn to the light that has never shone so brightly here. A place has come free, the struggle can begin, because the space will be occupied, by something or someone. It's like that for trees, it's like that for people.

Slow as a hearse, a truck that a tree trunk has been winched up onto drives through the streets, and people should overtake it with the same respect: calmly, without beeping. A veil of grief fell over Oucwègne that afternoon when its inhabitants saw that particular tree being carted off, as if Monsieur Potter was being buried for a second time. No signs of the cross were made and no heads were bared, but people's thoughts were gloomy and for a moment their stomachs felt empty. But a place had come free: with that tree Madame Verona was clearing away a big part of her past, to the well-concealed delight of every celibate. But that tree was going to return as a cello, they heard that soon enough from Charlo. There was no lover to smooth the path for them; it had not been a memento that needed clearing. Whereupon someone mumbled, roughly, 'If she doesn't watch out, she'll grow shut between the legs.' And it didn't occur to any of them that there might have been nothing else that could have made Madame Verona happier than being allowed to grow shut between the legs, to hold tight to what had once gone in that way.

XV

Pedants would chide her and tell her that she had made a home for herself in her own bad poem, where love is beyond time and space and even bigger, where existence has been uncoupled from all the laws that Newton and Co. ever racked their brains over, suggesting the unbearable conclusion that love was not part of existence. And yet... Still. For all that her lover had died, departed was a word she couldn't bring to bear. Although her ideas were far removed from the ones psychics had used many times to fleece the inconsolable – she *wanted* to be inconsolable –

they too came down to Monsieur Potter accompanying her wherever she went.

When she looked out the window at the valley, she looked with him. When she ate, she ate with him. That was partly why she never urged visitors to stay for dinner, preferring the intimacy of the idea and feeling of dining alone with her husband. Just the two of them, and a bottle that proceeded towards its original emptiness half as fast as before. She was aware that she sometimes spoke to him out loud in the process; it wasn't as if words slipped out to confront her with the pain of her loss. There was no madness at work here, there were never any complete conversations. It was short sentences. Now and then. 'Oh honey, a warm bath would do me the world of good.' Or, 'My student, Bossart, you remember, he played piano today as if he was typing out another essay.' Once again: she didn't expect him to jump up to run a bath for her, or entertain her by immediately giving an impression of a typist at a piano keyboard. She loved speaking in the tone she used to use when talking to him, a specific tone she had developed during their time together, a tone she had never adopted with anyone else and had come to miss in her voice. Missing him, she had begun to miss qualities of her own; revisiting them made him seem within reach.

She sought what others find in an embrace by putting on his clothes. Especially the baggy polo-neck jumpers he had taken to wearing after he started being embarrassed by the scar the removal of a bad mole had left on his neck. Of course she felt like she was making his death absolute the first time she put his jumpers in the washing machine, something she postponed for as long as possible, only to discover to her delight that his smell had survived the assault of the washing powder.

Of all the things that were still possible, this was her favourite: in the armchair, her nose buried under his turned-up collar, reading a book. After five pages she invariably wondered what she had just read but never considered flicking back to pick up the story.

It wasn't so much the reading she loved as the act of reading, sitting there in his clothes, as if sitting in him, and knowing that another day had become part of the past and she was enjoying, *with him*, the little time that people can spend in supreme uselessness.

The men of Oucwègne who came up to do odd jobs said the same thing, Monsieur Potter is still there in that house! Thriller writers who cater for the human need for fear would seize upon this fact as an opportunity to discuss ghosts and spectral illusions. Deploying all the stylistic devices they had at their disposal in an attempt to explain something whose only explanation lies in its inexplicableness. They were only too glad to come, the men of Oucwègne, and seized upon the leaking roof or broken lamp or whatever it might be as an alibi to test their charms, bringing up the subject of what a waste it was to be lonely. They always set out with firm resolve, but once they'd made it into the house their hearts were in their boots because – despite knowing little of love

– they knew enough to see that *here* Madame Verona was still living off the interest.

*

It was the nights, leaden and too long, that stood in the way of her illusions. The house stood ricketier and ricketier on its foundations and she knew that it would be a close call as to who needed renovating first, her or it. In bed she listened to things giving in to the wind: a roof tile, a flowerpot letting itself be pushed around the garden. But even when the wind didn't blow, the house creaked as if it was doing it of its own accord the way some people crack their knuckles to loosen their joints. If she had a stray dog in the house, at moments like these she hoped with all her heart that it felt at home and brave enough to bark or growl at anything it couldn't quite place in the echo chamber of its new surroundings. In the periods when she wasn't sheltering any dogs, she realized that she was counting on Monsieur Potter, who would get out of bed and go downstairs with heart pounding to make sure it wasn't burglars, something he had actually always known beforehand. She wasn't brave enough to go downstairs herself. And what if she did, and found herself eye to eye with a person of bad will, how would that lead to a better outcome? In moments like these her ideas about Monsieur Potter's presence were inadequate. He was dead. Dead dead. And he was dead when the thunderstorms aimed their stroboscopic lights at Oucwègne. Her powerlessness in the face of nature's rage was not diminished by his absence, no arms were able to lull her fear, not even his, but when he was still alive they had made a habit of going down the hill to get drunk whenever thunderstorms racked the night. They counted the devastating seconds between lightning and thunder as if that would make blind Fate turn away. Without him she couldn't find the courage to go down the hill and even her dogs proved useless. They crawled off into the smallest corners of the house, burying their heads under their paws in accordance with a philosophy that should in all fairness be attributed to more than just ostriches.

These storms reminded her that she was a girl from the north. People who had grown up in these hills were used to the clatter that came a couple of times a year to give nightmares to those who had been through the war. The big ones were announced by silence, the birds dropped the fioriture from their scores and joined the primordial hush. You saw the devastation approaching in the distance, the heavens spewing colours no child in the world would have grabbed out of the crayon box. The rumbling moved closer. Until finally the whole flotilla of clouds was hanging overhead for hours on end, making the village the plaything of a demented god. The heavens roared about all the things they had ever been or would ever be subjected to. No matter how many of her husband's jumpers she put on, it didn't help. During the most intense storms, she had sometimes, momentarily, considered seeking out the company of someone else, knocking on their door to say, 'Talk to me, drink with me, until the fury has passed.' But she was afraid of the false expectations she would arouse, and of the joviality of men who said, 'Just think of the flashes as a photo session. Smile!' Hard men who were allowed to be scared of nature, as long as they didn't admit it publicly.

*

In an increasingly isolated village she inhabited the most isolated house. And as far as anyone knew, it had always been inhabited by outsiders, people from elsewhere, who came here with a romantic view of isolation and paid for it later with large chunks of their mind. The villagers remembered a dreamer, almost a gypsy, who fired shots into the walls and ceilings while dancing around the rooms once madness had him in its nets. They recalled a woman who drank herself a miscarriage, hurled her empty bottles at the trees and was finally carted off in an ambulance to a place where she could go simple in pyjamas until the Lord stiffened her foolish grin and accepted her into His blissful flock. They started to repeat themselves, but no smile was safe for long in that house. Madame Verona would do well to abandon her hill, to move away. It wasn't loneliness that would soften her brains, she didn't suffer from that at all. It was the solitariness, which she refused to give up. She was alone and alone to stay. Because only alone can a person remember the person attuned to two.

XVI

Of all the reasons girls young and old have for lovingly and beautifully spreading their legs, playing the cello has received by far the least attention and here too precious little of that shortfall will be made up.

*

A life should last love's length and no longer, and a shiver passed through Madame Verona's body when they informed her that the second layer of varnish had been applied to her instrument, which was more or less to say that twenty years had passed since the felling of the tree. They had been the slowest years of her existence, cribbed from exhaustion and forced upon her by the dogs that kept getting lost until they found a new mistress to guard. But the years had passed, adding themselves to the mulch of the past, where they would still have a little time to compost into memory.

She had grown old, but not effortlessly, the way a book on a shelf grows old. She was old, definitely; she had had enough of everything, long since, and she realized she could grow even older. Another twenty years could easily be added to her life, thirty even, forty if Fortuna's caprice showed her no mercy. Mother Nature is like that; she picks out a few random creatures here and there to motivate the young to live even more recklessly out of disgust for decrepitude, and Madame Verona was increasingly suited to that macabre role.

She could still get up and down the hill, and would be able to manage it for a while yet. But she had started taking longer over the climb and paused more often on the way, resting her bags on the ground and gasping for breath. Each subsequent climb would be slower than the one before; the account had been opened, the tendency had become a certainty. Those who still regularly conversed had others to point out the start of their decline, flagged by the way they repeated themselves more quickly, forgetting what they had just said. Madame Verona only had herself to catch her out when, more and more often, she left the same sentences unsaid.

It wasn't the mirror that insulted her or the hair she found on her pillowcase in the morning, but her dreams, which, although renowned for being able to twist reality into a plausible unreality, were unable to succeed in making Monsieur Potter grow old with her. If she dreamed about him, and that wasn't something she looked forward to, it was as the man she had known. A young man. And the woman he took in his young arms in her dreams was her: an old woman. She found it repugnant. But the subconscious takes no offence at bad taste and never woke her before the dream had been dreamed to completion. She hated the illogicality of it. Love was the one and the many; she had thought that her lover growing old in time with her would have at least been dreamable.

Yes, it had come as a shock when the cello maker informed her that the instrument would be delivered to her home the next day. It wasn't so much the thinning out of the calendar that made her shudder as the fact that she had proved so capable of surviving without him these twenty years. It was the dogs that always came to offer themselves, almost as if they were doing it to give *her* the pleasure of caring for someone or something rather than to satisfy any needs of their own. If she was being honest, Madame Verona would admit that she had used that constant supply of dogs to stay alive, as if they were her only valid excuse. It was a betrayal – one no one would hold against her – of an alliance, of sacraments holier than marriage.

*

That cello: it was ugly, as expected. The hand of the craftsman was unmistakable, a master who had produced a minor miracle with the inferior materials foisted upon him. But compared with cellos made of the right kinds of wood, this was a monstrosity and she felt guilty towards the maker, who had worked on it for years in the full knowledge that this instrument was an insult to his talent. Of course, she had been warned and the warning had proved superfluous. She had known what to expect, but expectations arose to be disappointed, and that was why it hurt her so much to realize that for once they had been fulfilled so exactly. From scroll to tailpiece a failure, and as much a cello as a banjo can be a guitar.

She put the instrument in a corner of the room, unplayed, because if there was one thing she had few illusions about it was the sound. She was all too familiar with the vanity of luthiers, often justified, who were fond of playing a few bars for their customers. A little Boccherini, a touch of Bach. To demonstrate the sound, but at the same time wanting to prove that they were more than just cabinet-makers. As if to say, 'Hey, we quarter sawed the boards and let them dry. We went to check them every day, for years, mind you, and spoke to them as unabashedly as a gardener greeting his roses. We assembled this instrument with the utmost precision. And all because we know the beauty it serves. Listen.' With a careless hand they would brush aside all compliments about the excellence of their playing. 'Come now, you're exaggerating,' they would say, 'I'm just a simple carpenter,' preferring that word now even to luthier, seeing as it has often been carpenters who, in the fringes of the history of literature, have enjoyed the privilege of standing at the cradle of a miracle: Joseph, Geppetto. And meanwhile they puff up their chests with pride, ready to return home with a levity that will make their wives cheerful. But not once had this cello maker bowed the strings by way of demonstration; he hadn't even casually plucked a single string. One wondered whether he had even dared to test his merchandise in the work-shop, anxious perhaps to retain the benefit of the doubt.

Look in any reference book on the theory of music and it will tell you that, more than any other instrument, the cello is closest to the human voice. It doesn't take an especially developed ear to realize that this statement flatters the human voice. No shortage of ugly voices, but if there was one cello anywhere that could approach human croaking and droning, this would be it. The only thing was, who wanted to hear it?

*

The cello had stood there for weeks in a corner of the room, dead furniture, when Madame Verona suddenly opened the windows and took it between her legs.

The smell of rosin and all it evoked...

*

She bowed the strings for the first time, as if cutting someone's throat with a knife. People with a less misanthropic imagination might prefer to limit the simile to a mother cutting slices of bread – why not, that image too can be part of the reality. As long as it's cutting. She cut a second time, not even hoping she was mistaken, but to hear again what had never been in doubt: the ugly sound, the disappointing resonance, the miserable timbre. Perhaps she was looking for something beautiful in that ugliness – after all, ugly things often present that possibility – trying to find some way of turning the instrument's failings to her hand. Someone with a sarcastic disposition would have known what to do with this cello, that was obvious. Our characterization of Madame Verona in these pages has been careless if the immediate conclusion is that sarcasm was a thing she did not appreciate. She had no aversion to the sentiment and had, in the past, used it unsparingly. That was why she realized that sarcasm was a form of laziness, a house that was open to the unenlightened, and an emotion that would have been completely out of place in this situation.

She played. It sounded ugly, but she played. Fauré. The pieces she had played with her lover at the academy, but now her cheeks weren't red. She pressed herself tight against the instrument to feel the vibrations. And if she closed her eyes, it was not to enjoy the results of her own fingering, but to hear the piano that Monsieur Potter would have played to accompany her. That was how she would do it every evening from now on. She would sit at the window with legs spread and play the cello. An ensemble that wasn't, a duet with absence. Talking to the nonexistent, which might be the only correct definition of very deep prayer.

XVII

There are but few occasions on which it is permissible to use the phrase 'fatal day' and a littérateur worth his salt would seize them with both hands. In this case, however, he would be exaggerating and drawing attention to his own bluff. It was true that fatal days could begin with radio reports of imminent and heavy snow; ask any film director. They could easily begin the way this February day began: with a few council workers taking the precaution of closing the difficult hill road, dragging on their fags, then treating themselves to a break in the back of the van, sharing the provisions their wives had wrapped in cling film and poured into thermoses for them that morning.

Madame Verona had got up without plans and was greeted by her tail-wagging dog. She had eaten breakfast with the radio on and heard what she herself could have predicted with considerably less effort, that there would be a momentous snowfall that would make the roads virtually impassable. It was often like that in late February: encouraged by the slowly lengthening days, birds cautiously sung their territories, trees budded and creatures that had buried themselves for the winter got ready to be reunited with the sun. And that was the very moment the winter slammed in one last time, to purge the world of idiots. Toads, horny as hell, that began their nocturnal marches when it was moist and around eight degrees, were able to meet their maker without even needing a car to squash them. The last, bitter winter offensive was a death sentence for premature joie de vivre, existence was reserved for those who always arrived everywhere a little too late. Only mankind shepherded its idiots through winter's last attack, offering up a handful of flu-bitten pensioners in exchange.

After listening to the weather report, Madame Verona washed herself, but not like someone who is expected somewhere. And then she lit the fire as carefully as an enthusiastic Brownie jockeying for Brown Owl's approval. Of course she had watched her woodpile shrink to an alarming minimum and her mind had raced as she carried the last ten pieces of wood inside in a basket. But it wasn't until she was pushing the last log into the fire that she drew her conclusion, calmly, in complete tranquillity. She put on her coat, which confused the dog but also cheered him up, glad as he was to interrupt his daily routine with a walk.

She had always taken her dogs out hiking with her, all except this one. This one had come into her life after abandoning his farmyard in a lather of lust, searching for a partner for a quick mate and losing his good sense and the way back in the process. And seizing the opportunity to find a better master. Judging by his appetite he had been on the road for days, and the sleep that he finally gave in to after his meal lasted for days as well, interrupted only occasionally by his turning over with a sigh. When he awoke from it, he immediately placed himself at the service of his hostess, making this clear by barking at postmen and pigeons that dared to alight on the terrace. No one missed him; the animal shelter hadn't had anyone drop by looking for their great lump of a dog, and the posters that occasionally adorned the streets, hung up mainly by dejected children, only ever showed snaps of permed, almost woollen little doggies.

Madame Verona was willing to let him stay, as long as he realized his future grave would not be located in a corner of the garden of this house. It was a temporary solution, considering his youth. He didn't need to entertain any illusions about going for walks with Madame Verona as well. He had a garden and it was big enough for him to stretch his legs and relieve himself in. The animal had long since resigned himself to the course of events, which explains his surprise when Madame Verona, after adding the last piece of wood to the fire, put on her coat and beckoned him to the door. The prospect of finally being able to empty his shrunken bladder on posts, letterboxes and car wheels elicited his most charming bark and would have had him ramming his mistress's legs with joy except that he realized she was too old for that kind of doggery, and that it would most likely lead to his having the implantation of a plastic hip on his conscience.

*

They walked. It was slow, but they walked. From the door to the forest path. The steep forest path. Many people would have looked back one last time, casting a last glance at the house. The site of love and mourning. Not Madame Verona. She took another step downhill. Ten paces later she turned to call the dog, which had stayed standing on the hilltop as if he, the shepherd, had realized very well that she would never make it back up. But she called him and he followed her, after a bark that could have been his last.

We know that, after reaching the valley, they sat down on a bench. We know that it started to snow. And we know that Madame Verona finally permitted herself a short walk to warm up a little, and that the dog followed her again. Her journey ended under the plane tree on the village square, the location of the pétanque field which had given rise to decades of discussions about vitally important millimetres. Where the river took up the singing men's froth and the smell of frying fish attracted stray cats. She sat down on one of the rocks and could imagine how much she would have enjoyed a cigarette at that moment, although she had never smoked. Pity, a packet of her husband's was still up at the house.

The dog lay down on her feet, either from

helpfulness, hoping to transform himself into an extra pair of socks for his increasingly hypothermic mistress, or from fear. It didn't help having Madame Verona say to him every now and then, 'Go away, boy! Go find a home!' He stayed lying there, more faithful in the face of death than she herself had ever had the courage to be. And who was she to give him a kick to get rid of him? Maybe a car would stop after all to present them with a lift. In that case Madame Verona would stay sitting, no question of that, but offer the people the dog. That possibility was the only thing she had left to anticipate. Beyond it lay the Nothing we can all imagine ourselves one day entering with a sense of déjà vu. The last moments of a life, and she found it no strain at all to think once again about her lover. Just a little bit longer and that Nothing would embrace her, but with arms that could also be his. That was how a smile came to be found in the morning, frozen on a face that was turned to the realm of fables. The face of someone who is greeting a doorman and proceeding to a front desk where she will answer the most important question by saying that she has been lucky enough to attract dogs, her whole life long.

To find out more about our books, to meet our authors, to discover new writing, to get inspiration for your book group, to read exclusive on-line interviews, blogs and comment, and to sign up for our newsletter, visit **www.portobellobooks.com**

encouraging voices,
supporting writers,
challenging readers

Portobello
BOOKS